CAN ANYBODY HEAR ME?

Jessica Meserve

Andersen Press

This is Jack. He is very quiet.

This is Jack's family. They are **VERY NOISY**.
In fact, they are so noisy that
no one seems to hear Jack.

Jack said to Ma, "I'm going to the mountain today."

Ma said, "One or two pancakes?"

Jack said, "One, please." Ma gave him two.

Jack said to Granny and Gramps,
"I'm going to walk to the top of the mountain today."

Granny said, "I'm going to knit you a nice
new sweater. What colour, red or blue?"

Jack said, "Blue, please."

Granny said, "Red is a very good choice."

Gramps said, "I'm going to write a song about red."

Jack said to Pa,
"I'm going to the very top of the mountain today."

Pa said, "Are you going fishing in the creek?"

Jack said, "No, I'm going to the mountain."

Pa said, "Catch some big ones."

Jack said to June-bug and Jim-bob,
"Do you want to come to the top of the moutain?"

June-bug said to Jim-bob,
"Jack wants to play hide-and-seek."

Jack said, "No, I want to go to the mountain."

Jim-bob said,
"Count to fifty, Jack. We'll hide."

"I wonder if anybody heard me say I'm going to the
mountain," thought Jack. "I hope someone did."
He set off on his own with just his best friend,
Chester for company.

Past the barn.
Across the pastures
and over the whooshing,
burbling waterfall.

Up, up, up the mountain side . . .

. . . until he reached
the top of the mountain.

The mountain top was still and quiet.
Jack took a deep breath, filled his
lungs and shouted with all his might.

"Can anybody hear me?"

Jack barely heard his voice fill the silence
for a second before it disappeared into
the vast sky around him.

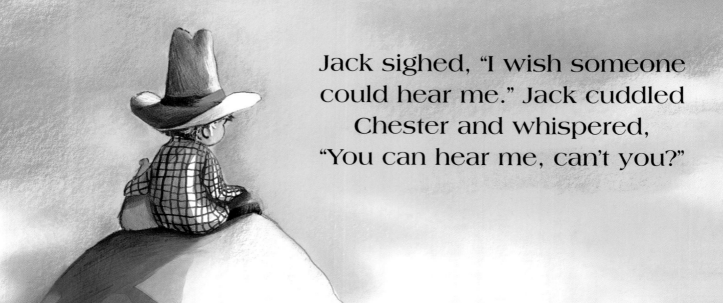

Jack sighed, "I wish someone could hear me." Jack cuddled Chester and whispered, "You can hear me, can't you?"

"Yes," said Chester, looking straight at him. "I have always heard you."

Jack blinked with surprise, then smiled
and said, "Do you want to play?"

Chester smiled back and said, "Yes."

Together they slid down the
snowy peak of the mountain
and fell giggling into a heap
of snow.

At the bottom of the slope
they found a young wolf-cub all alone.
"Do you think he's lost?" asked Jack.

"Yes," said Chester. "We should
call for his mother. Maybe if we
howl together, she'll hear us."

Jack was doubtful.
"No one ever seems to hear me."

"I can," said Chester.
"Give it a go!"

Ow Ow Aw ooooooooo ooooo

Ow Ow Aw ooooooooo ooooooo ooooo

Ow Ow Aw ooooooooo oo

Ow Ow Aw ooooooooo oo

So together they howled like wolves.

Soon, over the hill, a much larger wolf
bounded towards them.

"There," said Chester,
"I knew you could do it."
Together they walked
down the mountain side
towards home.

Suddenly, a bear appeared on the path, towering above them. Jack and Chester froze.

Chester's voice quivered. "If you look big and growl back, you can scare him away," he said.

Jack's legs were shaking, but he took a deep breath, filled his lungs and growled his biggest growl.

Grrrrrrrrrrrrrrrrrrrrrr

The bear fled into the woods.

Chester smiled. "You were
very fierce and loud."

Jack smiled back. "Thank you."

Night fell.
"Chester," Jack said.
"I think we're lost."

"If you can call a mother wolf
and scare away a bear, you
can yell for help," said Chester.

Jack picked up Chester. He took a
deep breath, filling his lungs,
and shouted out,

"Can anybody hear me?"

Only an owl hooted in response. "I think I'm still not noisy enough for *my* family to hear me," said Jack.

But then Jack saw lanterns bobbing in the distance.
He heard the voices of Ma and Pa.

"Jack, where are you?"
"Jack, can you hear us?"

Jack called with all his might,
"I'm over here, I'm over here!"

The voices of his family drew closer.

Jack smiled. "They can hear me, Chester.
Just like you."

Pa cried, "We were so worried! No one knew where you were."

"Chester knew where I was," Jack said.

"Chester?" Pa laughed.

"Come on, it's time for supper," said Ma.

Chester winked at Jack.

Back at the ranch,
Jack's family all talked at
once, asking where he had
been. Jack took a deep breath,
filling his lungs, and with his biggest
voice he shouted, "QUIET, PLEASE!"
His family became as quiet as mice.
Then Jack began his story, and this time
they all heard EVERY WORD.